# A CHILD'S CALENDAR

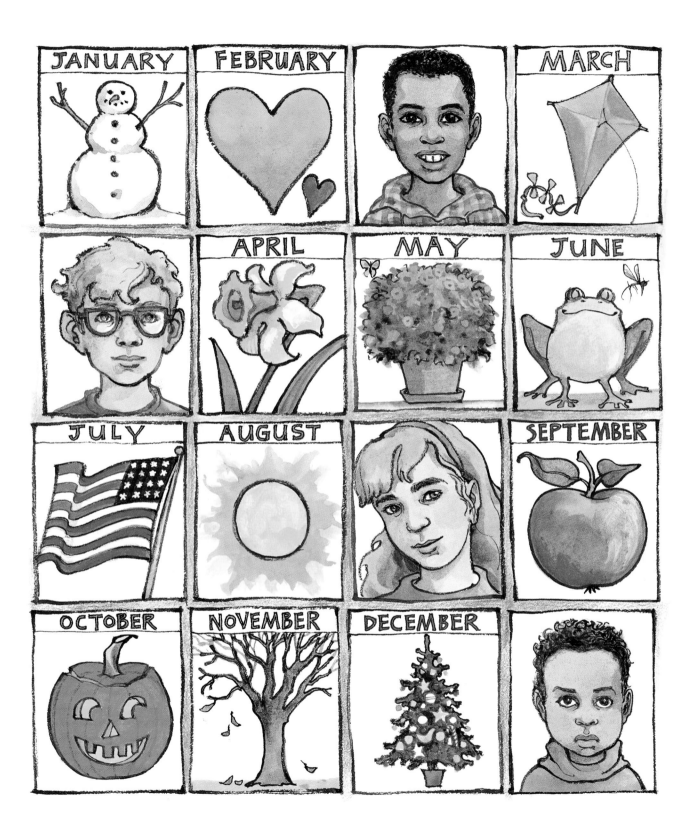

JANUARY
FEBRUARY
MARCH
APRIL
MAY
JUNE
JULY
AUGUST
SEPTEMBER
OCTOBER
NOVEMBER
DECEMBER

# A
# CHILD'S
# CALENDAR

*Poems by*

## JOHN UPDIKE

*Illustrations by*

## TRINA SCHART HYMAN

HOLIDAY HOUSE

New York

Printed and bound February 2017 at Tien Wah Press, Johor Bahru, Johor, Malaysia.

A CHILD'S CALENDAR was published first
by Alfred A. Knopf, Inc. in 1965,
with illustrations by Nancy Ekholm Burkert.
The text for this new edition incorporates
a number of changes
by the author.

Library of Congress Cataloging-in-Publication Data
Updike, John.
A child's calendar/by John Updike;
illustrated by Trina Schart Hyman.
p.   cm.
Summary: A collection of twelve poems
describing the activities in a child's life and the changes
in the weather as the year moves from January to December.
ISBN-13: 978-0-8234-1445-1 (hardcover)
ISBN-13: 978-0-8234-1766-7 (paperback)
1. Months—Juvenile poetry. 2. Children's poetry, American.
[1. Months—Poetry. 2. American poetry.]
I. Hyman, Trina Schart, ill. II. Title. PS3571.P4C49
1999 811'.54—dc21   98–46166
CIP   AC

11 13 15 17 19 20 18 16 14 12

HOLIDAY HOUSE is registered in the U.S. Patent and Trademark office.

To Liz and Miranda
—J. U.

To Michou and Xavier
—T. S. H.

# A CHILD'S CALENDAR

# January

The days are short,
　　The sun a spark
Hung thin between
　　The dark and dark.

Fat snowy footsteps
　　Track the floor,
And parkas pile up
　　Near the door.

The river is
　　A frozen place
Held still beneath
　　The trees' black lace.

The sky is low.
　　The wind is gray.
The radiator
　　Purrs all day.

# February

The sun rides higher
   Every trip.
The sidewalk shows.
   Icicles drip.

A snowstorm comes,
   And cars are stuck,
Though road salt flies
   From the old town truck.

The chickadees
   Grow plump on seed
That Mother pours
   Where they can feed,

And snipping, snipping
   Scissors run
To cut out hearts
   For everyone.

# March

The sun is nervous
  As a kite
That can't quite keep
  Its own string tight.

Some days are fair,
  And some are raw.
The timid earth
  Decides to thaw.

Shy budlets peep
  From twigs on trees,
And robins join
  The chickadees.

Pale crocuses
  Poke through the ground
Like noses come
  To sniff around.

The mud smells happy
  On our shoes.
We still wear mittens,
  Which we lose.

# April

It's spring! Farewell
   To chills and colds!
The blushing, girlish
   World unfolds

Each flower, leaf,
   And blade of turf—
Small love-notes sent
   From air to earth.

The sky's a herd
   Of prancing sheep,
The birds and fields
   Abandon sleep,

And jonquils, tulips,
   Daffodils
Bloom bright upon
   The wide-eyed hills.

All things renew.
   All things begin.
At church, they bring
   The lilies in.

# May

Now children may
　　Go out of doors,
Without their coats,
　　To candy stores.

The apple branches
　　And the pear
May float their blossoms
　　Through the air,

And Daddy may
　　Get out his hoe
To plant tomatoes
　　In a row,

And, afterwards,
　　May lazily
Look at some baseball
　　On TV.

# June

The sun is rich
   And gladly pays
In golden hours,
   Silver days,

And long green weeks
   That never end.
School's out. The time
   Is ours to spend.

There's Little League,
   Hopscotch, the creek,
And, after supper,
   Hide-and-seek.

The live-long light
   Is like a dream,
And freckles come
   Like flies to cream.

**JOHN UPDIKE** was born in 1932 in Shillington, Pennsylvania, and studied at Harvard College and the Ruskin School of Drawing and Fine Art in Oxford, England. The author of more than forty books, his works include collections of short stories, poems, and criticism. His novels have won the Pulitzer Prize, the National Book Award, and the National Book Critics Circle Award. He lives in Massachusetts.

**TRINA SCHART HYMAN** was born in 1939 in Philadelphia, Pennsylvania, and attended the Philadelphia College of Art, the Boston Museum School of Fine Arts, and the School for Applied Art in Stockholm, Sweden. She has illustrated more than one hundred books for children. Her work has received the Caldecott Medal, Caldecott Honor awards, and the Boston Globe-Horn Book Award. She lives in New Hampshire.

# December

First snow! The flakes,
   So few, so light,
Remake the world
   In solid white.

All bundled up,
   We feel as if
We were fat penguins,
   Warm and stiff.

The toy-packed shops
   Half split their sides,
And Mother brings home
   Things she hides.

Old carols peal.
   The dusk is dense.
There is a mood
   Of sweet suspense.

The shepherds wait,
   The kings, the tree—
All wait for something
   Yet to be,

Some miracle.
   And then it's here,
Wrapped up in hope—
   Another year!

# November

The stripped and shapely
   Maple grieves
The loss of her
   Departed leaves.

The ground is hard,
   As hard as stone.
The year is old,
   The birds are flown.

And yet the world,
   Nevertheless,
Displays a certain
   Loveliness—

The beauty of
   The bone. Tall God
Must see our souls
   This way, and nod.

Give thanks: we do,
   Each in his place
Around the table
   During grace.

# October

The month is amber,
   Gold, and brown.
Blue ghosts of smoke
   Float through the town,

Great V's of geese
   Honk overhead,
And maples turn
   A fiery red.

Frost bites the lawn.
   The stars are slits
In a black cat's eye
   Before she spits.

At last, small witches,
   Goblins, hags,
And pirates armed
   With paper bags,

Their costumes hinged
   On safety pins,
Go haunt a night
   Of pumpkin grins.

# September

The breezes taste
　Of apple peel.
The air is full
　Of smells to feel—

Ripe fruit, old footballs,
　Drying grass,
New books and blackboard
　Chalk in class.

The bee, his hive
　Well-honeyed, hums
While Mother cuts
　Chrysanthemums.

Like plates washed clean
　With suds, the days
Are polished with
　A morning haze.

# August

The sprinkler twirls.
   The summer wanes.
The pavement wears
   Popsicle stains.

The playground grass
   Is worn to dust.
The weary swings
   Creak, creak with rust.

The trees are bored
   With being green.
Some people leave
   The local scene

And go to seaside
   Bungalows
And take off nearly
   All their clothes.

# July

Bang-*bang*! Ka-*boom*!
 We celebrate
Our national
 Independence date,

The Fourth, with
 Firecrackers and
The marching of
 The Legion Band.

America:
 It makes us think
Of hot dogs, fries,
 And Coke to drink.

The shade is hot.
 The little ants
Are busy, but
 Poor Fido pants

And Tabby dozes
 In a pool
Of fur she sheds
 To keep her cool.